## ALSO BY JOHN ASHBERY

POETRY

Turandot and Other Poems

Some Trees

The Tennis Court Oath

Rivers and Mountains

The Double Dream of Spring

Three Poems

The Vermont Notebook

Self-Portrait in a Convex Mirror

Houseboat Days

As We Know

Shadow Train

A Wave

Selected Poems

April Galleons

Flow Chart

Hotel Lautréamont

And the Stars Were Shining

Can You Hear, Bird

Wakefulness

The Mooring of Starting Out:
The First Five Books of Poetry

Girls on the Run

Your Name Here

As Umbrellas Follow Rain

Chinese Whispers

Where Shall I Wander

A Worldly Country

Notes from the Air:
Selected Later Poems

Collected Poems, 1956–1987

Planisphere

Quick Question

FICTION

A Nest of Ninnies
(with James Schuyler)

PLAYS

Three Plays

CRITICISM AND ESSAYS

Reported Sightings:
Art Chronicles, 1957–1987

Other Traditions (The Charles
Eliot Norton Lectures)

Selected Prose

# BREEZEWAY

# JOHN ASHBERY

# Breezeway

NEW POEMS

An Imprint of HarperCollinsPublishers

HarperCollins books may be purchased for educational, business, or sales promotional use. For information please e-mail the Special Markets Department at SPsales@harpercollins.com.

A hardcover edition of this book was published in 2015 by Ecco, an imprint of HarperCollins Publishers.

FIRST ECCO PAPERBACK EDITION PUBLISHED 2016.

Designed by Quemadura
This book is printed on Earthchoice Tradebook Freesheet

Library of Congress Cataloging-in-Publication Data has been applied for.

ISBN 978-0-06-238704-2

16 17 18 19 20   QK/RRD   10 9 8 7 6 5 4 3 2 1

FOR DAVID KERMANI

# BREEZEWAY

## THE DREAM OF A RAREBIT FIEND

The fifty-foot old masterpiece, that awful necklace, is that good for you? I mean, do you like it any better? Treestumps?

Oh, Mr. Salteena, dear, it's good before anything else is. We're not opening today. Her intentional steel embrace scuttled it. Which is not to say you're not to proceed. On the contrary, we like you more than when we were at school, we and they. There are good times in everybody's satchel, nor do we all get a free pass. That would be a split decision, as they call it. How else is the planned brotherhood to float forward?

Watch her—she'll donate a medal to the crowd for a flag. It's why we call each other members. If we can get this stuff out of here, a little bit more power in the shins will come to seem appropriate. That's your cue. Don't let on I was here, helping with the tables sometimes. Ah it was awful the way they rushed him, past us and a few stragglers. We had been told to meet up with destiny at a corner of the fairgrounds, a pearl in fragments. It's so fun. A dollop here, a mess of particles there. Not everyone sees it as you do, which is right for them, no matter what territory they own and at times wander back to, unthinking, forgetting if a lurid sky can be just one thing, or under certain conditions definitive.

Why I never . . .

## THE SAD THING

He has a lazy father in Minnesota.

I hope you never have to do this in life, with its crazy little darkened rooms. People are standing, an accurate jumble. *Famille rose* happy campers.

And if the water tastes funny, she must be pretty young. That came from a tree.

# CHINESE FIRE DRILL

OK, I said it. Sarabande. A dance no one dances anymore. Except maybe in heaven, where they don't have better things to do. These clucks behind a fence . . . Now, of course, I'll have passed it on differently. They're here, instead of just wondering what they're doing. Gotta keep the red onion.

You move a lot in a cab. Not to stand up and eat their community. A few scheduling disasters later the daughters came down to lift us off the shore. We were branded with the name Lot. The waves beat them to it. We renounced our offshore inheritance. Oh, what difference does it make when the most mutable among us augment the mystery beyond all proportion, so as to accept the thanks that ingratitude inevitably trails in its wake. For whatever reason.

## SEVEN-YEAR-OLD AUROCH LIKES THIS

Will research tell us tomorrow
of normal morals? Take a Brooklyn family
in fracture mode, vivid,
energizing, throbs to the earlobes. Thanks
to a snakeskin toupee, my grayish push boots
exhale new patina/prestige. Exeunt the Kardashians.
Exit the emergency room. A nifty looking broad
goes up to a goofy guy. (There's the leader with its bow.)
Well, I wouldn't do it instantly. I'll bring you some,
uh, and well I'm dried.

Antique mud wrestlers shape up
for the last time, no scuttling of vain things
left undone. When you get back I'll just
hit another menu, safe as a can of soup
in a mini-mart.
Saw you first on *Masterpiece Theater*.
I used to climb right in. That was funny yet unbidden.
When you were alive they called him a stooge.
My voice to young adolescents is like, whom d'ya know,
hiding their accomplishments in bread?

Will keep on looking for birds of prey.
Sunbonnet Sue ought to be learning/lurking
flinging bridges across enormous spaces, the way
the Druids did. Perhaps Ottomans, now
that they've shrunk.
Mine's the control and I must deal with it.
Had a little discussion, benches throughout for safety.

We walked all the way here in the eighteenth century.
Century of closures! I'm not sure of that though.
Begin marinating and be out of here a whole bunch.
O melted butter! The devalued son looks up other people's
calisthenics, like that's going to change anything,
close himself to waking up, bodies not noticed.
As for the father, well, he'll become hybrid, like most of us,
who you walk along in grayness, against.

The salt has lost its savior.
*J'accuse.*

## DANS LE MÉTRO

*Miracle sans nom à la station Javel ...*
CHARLES TRENET, "Y a d'la joie"

We got in on the bottom line
at Duck Alley. Ten feet of onions to hoe
and a disruptive sneeze blew in
from the Sissy Isles. What I hope to say ...
What I hope to say is, out here west
of the water tower, waggish, resourceful,
you hardly walk away anymore.

At one of the president's meetings
(Miss Hazel to you) to oppose the new constitution
I thought you'd like to know about the pictures
of the babysitter. Tragic annals, rife again.
I was thinking of Tuesday night and none
of the background. I hope he feels good.

Late in the house, watched by my grandmother's
permanent low-grade calceolarias, sure

to come back breathless . . . It's all set up.
Strangers at a concession may find they
missed the onion maze phase of the celebrity mash-up.

The open system showing its age, they said.

Holy Grail, Batman! Can't *you* see it?
Ice cream fell on his arm when I went to explore
and found students reading papers. Please
join the opera about interesting things.
Congressman, I was one of the reasons the troubled
muse shuns its classical heritage. A positive negative voice.
Russell Weed said to read it,
and that's my weakness now.

                        What kind of machine
instructs his stiffening member?
That would help. I don't think I know who he is.
Like a disoriented codfish, the drive's
out to get me. Did I mention cockchafers?
I was quite different then,
guilty of changing the money. Look, I—
Thanks. So you can do this at home,
on a whoopee calendar. But don't do that.

                                    Sleeping
with naked eyebrows, they didn't realize they weren't
modern. And such was the result.
But he never forgot that day on the water.
That, and mutability issues. *Capisce?*

I *was* quite different then.
Yes, I just remembered.
She's going to be brutally named after you.
His shadow is on the other door.
What you see is what you get, neither
more nor less, but shapely.

Ratcheting up the task forces,
he'd hate yours.
Tell me. I'd assumed you were a doctor,
and it wasn't just the beautiful and exacting places.
Worries, I had a few, but everything looked distinct
in his calm lens. I kind of forgot why I was coming,
what I wanted to say, in Indian August especially.

Ripe stairs, staggered deaths,
board of humiliation, and they come in here—
the Ice Saints, big time tumblers.
She hardly touched her dinner: routine evangelism,
full of the luck we had just inherited,
the uncrazy things that happened
on your doorstep.

# THE WELKIN

We're patching up an agreement today.
The insides won't let us. I sent you copies
by return mail anytime soon.
We came to a long Q and A period,
to which dreams are the smutty alternative.
Of these by far the most startling
(not to be tedious) combat greasiness
from Calexico to Texarkana, a splash
on everything they do. They can't fit it in.

I long to talk with some old lover's ghost.
I don't try to understand anything
except our hat should be annoyed.
The shoreline goo stretched far away,
struggled to be determined
at least several times.

It came up before the present house.
I grew up there. The ground was still broken
around it. Have a dish from the legacy.
You're going to be good with that.

Ever since he took those vitamins a gag order
without any support for these
made five in the back seat.

They say it's infectious—
work stoppage, invisible mending afoot
that is a circa gritty one
backing through town,
allowed to have lunch if they don't want it.

Once-dirty glasses. Summit Valley.
I can't tell the doctor about it.

# CITY OF BOUNCERS

There's the speed of golden ivy,
the city wing. A hundred this weekend
having wonderful meeting, not slamming,
substantiated enough.
                        Where there's feet,
the not-so-air-conditioned gent in the foyer
invites you to a chop-busting. That will
patch up today's industrious pose
till the paint dries. Yes, and what about *you*
and your project? Afraid it'll grow beyond
the sustainable frontier, just like your Maw
warned you back in the day, when sisters
alighted from planes looking breezy and collected?

Putting it on the take with the haircut
I just limned, the event horizon
ought to be in fine shape by tomorrow.
Look, we just want to cancel our order.
Is that such a big deal, Danny boy?

## A BREAKFAST RADISH

Whatever we're dealing with catches us
in mid-reconsideration. It's beautiful,
my lord, just not made to be repeated,
that's all.

Counterterrorists have already invaded parts of England
and Spain. Your action dollar at work.
Deception figures in quite a few precious things,
although, as I say, it's a small remnant
of what others have achieved to avoid being singed.

We have a special on revenge tragedy.
March is going to be a heavier day.
The girls talked about getting ready.
When they do, in this or that glen,
looks can be deceiving, he shared.

# BREEZEWAY

Someone said we needed a breezeway
to bark down remnants of super storm Elias jugularly.
Alas it wasn't my call.
I didn't have a call or anything resembling one.
You see I have always been a rather dull-spirited winch.
The days go by and I go with them.
A breeze falls from a nearby tower,
finds no breezeway, goes away
along a mission to supersize red shutters.

Alas if that were only all.
There's the children's belongings to be looked to
if only one can find the direction needed
and stuff like that.
I said we were all homers not homos
but my voice dwindled in the roar of Hurricane Edsel.
We have to live out our precise experimentation.
Otherwise there's no dying for anybody,
no crisp rewards.

Batman came out and clubbed me.
He never did get along with my view of the universe

except you know existential threads
from the time of the peace beaters and more.
He patted his dog Pastor Fido.
There was still so much to be learned
and even more to be researched.
It was like a goodbye. Why not accept it,
anyhow? The mission girls came through the woods
in their special suitings. It was all whipped cream and baklava.
Is there a Batman somewhere, who notices us
and promptly looks away, at a new catalog, say,
or another racing car expletive
coming back at Him?

## LISTENING TOUR

We were arguing about whether NBC
was better than CBS. I said CBS
because it's smaller and had to work
harder to please viewers. You didn't
like either that much but preferred
smaller independent companies.
Just then an avalanche flew
overhead, light blue against the
sky's determined violet. We
started to grab our stuff but
it was too late. We segued . . .

And in another era the revolutions
were put down by the farmers,
working together with the peasants
and the enlightened classes. All
benefited in some way. That was
all I had to hear.
Whatever . . .

## HAND WITH A PICTURE

Here's what we haven't done yet.
I'll remember that morning temperature.
Meanwhile I'm cautiously optimistic.

That afternoon in bed
on the big farm
was one of those times,
whether we need it.

The hem of her story in the edge,
funny loaves to wash it down with,
too much or too little sleep—
do we have any place to sit?

I haven't even got time to talk to you yet.
Saw vision ahead of me. Yes I can't find it now,
the work history. What's it called?

Do you want us to eliminate
the few times it makes me feel great?
In ways that you don't know? Neither
conspicuously handsome nor precisely plain, the ego

seemed to dote on its imperfections,
giggling at thunderstorms,
at balding consciousness.
I know just how you must feel about it.
I'm outta here.

News every day, or distressing silences.
A dish in a respected room.
The one who was coming back, arguing
back and forth, hit the wrong bathroom —
A power hugely shifting at bottom
to wander on that floor . . .

## A GREETING TO MY BROTHERS AND
## SOME OF MY BROTHERS-IN-LAW

The chic flatness of memory
takes the arctic brotherhood to task.
Where'd you get it at?
Don't think of it yet.
Awake in the shadow of the school's cactus garden
you have ALL of the handcuffs,
bracelets, whatever,
like the exploding manhole covers of Skopje.

How open was it?
To here a former first lady,
the victims were visited too and
down there for ten days without a punchline.
He's only got seven kids and none of these are tea drinkers.
Restrictions led the way,
then grunge too passed, leaving a dimpled wake
much prized by amateurs.
What to reoffer? Wow.
Suddenly a giant snowflake pierced the trellis
thirty-five minutes ago, trapped in honey.

So.
You've been asleep
because he remembers it.
Now I'm supposed to be here.

## LEAF, RESTING

What do you insist.
I'm so happy that
it was then that
a lot of them prefer it better. Yes.

And *now* he's gonna learn it to us
like we were supposed to. *Damn!*
And maybe you weren't that cocksure
a weekend they were checked in and out of the gas station.

O higher than the grave,
always aware, under the occasion,
what kind of peace I don't know.
We're not gonna be here anymore.

It may not be the same thing: ghost-published.
Liquidational. Then I wrote my Minuet in G.
Help you guys. The kind of messages we read
on the surfaces of certain clouds.

I remember last night I told you what happened,
or the . . . incubator. The response has been lousy,
a veiled, intense gaze, that could have as easily . . .
It broke your sister's heart.

## MRS. FOSTER'S PEARS

He said she was partially undressed.
It turned out neither knew the other's race.
Well, his dad says he was set up.
He began to record other people.

I've got a doctor's appointment Friday
not dinner for quite a while,
and where it happened,
my silver dear. Or ear,
my sled less than a newborn stove
in his office somewhere.

Now he's scouting it,
the date on the drawer.

These are interesting to me.
Take a close look.
Alarmingly, the two sides had come together.
Let's just say there are people in there.
His father didn't laugh in this manner

who failed all night
and didn't let us know when it was ready.

What crumbles before it crumbles?
An abundance of samples.

# ANDANTE AND FILIBUSTER

Remember last month, when he was saying
doomed lovers' syndrome uproots us all?
They all wanna hear that,
and hanging them out to dry slumpingly caresses
the center for new needs, and we'll stiffen some near
the walled city and find 100 percent electricity of the vote.

(Not sure about *that*.) Funny you should ask.
We got a small grant to have the house inspected and
as a result of that discovered a small crack
leading from the front door to the basement.
Much thinner air here, although the nation's salt and pepper
sprinkle the neighborhood. Hose her down. Keep trying
to creep out, test ingot possibilities.
Recently in the stores I spotted
preppy garbage. Grew a ten-gallon hat shopping
in the ruins, how it feels around
the edges—something you do for a moment. Brutally
obnoxious, I like to know who's coming and going
and not be bothered. (Promised

to wake him up in July.) Still not doing
anything to incur our attention?

Then you have followed all what we have to say.
Cough it up—little green cross-eyed slots.
No bricks. Just mortar. Ready. Ready for a takeover.
The catalpas of reconciliation wilt,
proving, if little else,
why a good presentation matters.

We talked about the great error
that you can live with
and really can't afford to get.
It's Thanksgiving there, and besides
we might not have room for the next event
to get the old juices flowing.

A gay avalanche destroyed much of the town.
Please, I thought we were winning.
Set the wolves, I mean the dogs
on her, that is, him.
The stalled investigation proved otherwise.
And give back the taxpayers' money.
The space program cost too much anyway.

Al and Harry had their moment in the sun.
Oblivion swiftly followed, the universe
playing catch-up, as
it is wont to do. Oh, bugger
the attendance record! I see a long line

of attendees waiting, cock in hand.
She thought it was lumbago.
The handwriting on the wainscot pledged otherwise.

All came from today backgrounds.
A fistful of s'mores
put death itself on the agenda
for future discussion.
How does that break down?
Minutes happening . . . I don't think so.
You stepping all over the sprinkles.

## BY THE BYPASS

Pucker your ankles. Don't freeze the weapons, or
at this hour a lot of places are going to be cooling down.
It's going to the fireside. Until things get better.
They would never have anything to do with finding real estate,
get to me through sheer sense of place.
                                        Three days packing fog,
abducted, later released, she doesn't know how to get here.
The same feeling is appealing, it's disruptive when
our fans get ahead. Those who help me understood
henbane is box office poison. Same for midlength weepies.
Those who understand them don't necessarily understand,
nor play favorites when the other children are near.
You tittered, like, is there something I'm not getting here?
Oh shut up and do it.

He took advantage of her/me.
What is that like in your life?
It could never have happened.
Come with me somewhere.

## STRANGE REACTION

Our networks will be joining you in progress.
Let's break for lunch here, dry-eyed,
alarming, and see what everybody's talking about.
We can always resume our travels for what they are,
and if that is so, if they're fun and expensive,
why not number them? Things sag if you make them,
or not. Elders give up

within the appointed time — Get your lifestyle together
or something, miles from here, much of it downstairs.
Go lie on the couch. Why, you scheming . . . From the cast-iron
villas of the sanctimonious to the feathered huts
of the poor in spirit, a hush fringed all night.

Dawn put in her two cents.
By then we were deep in imagination.
Storks and secretary birds rose in a single wave,
charming in its generality. A pink jumper
stroked the trees. So, where were you?
This was it? What we got all cleaned up for?
Tomorrow will rob today of croutons, I don't think.

# TALL ORDER

The narrative got punctured.
On a rainy night you can spot a missionary,
though I don't think it's stupid enough to get lathered up about.
The revenooers came after the affordables
and all was *durcheinander*, like I say
it was. Burn every newspaper in the country,

but if that's not possible, well,
I'll keep it between my legs
or some other barnyard denizen.
It was him who got into some scrape yesterday.
We knew all along he had followed the corrugated path
picking up crumbs like there was no tomorrow, which
there isn't. But as long as you're here
we may as well begin.

# BOTCHED ROLLOUT

Friends of the Tao curtail fancy matters.
Are you an in-depth person? Proud and sad?
OK, I'll be pleasant. That's how I kind of fixed it.
Both of our kids were unlikeable characters.

I could hear you perfectly with the shades drawn,
you big man. Two sisters, one permanently
claims, with a bit of practice, the high estate
behind smilax. She's plain. Very collectible. So the estimate

bill can go directly to him, heading home from work.
Is that little brain you've given me ever going to ring,
that piece of arrogance? Which way to the weep-in?
The act of repositioning downward has been pretty much mothballed,

so I would tell the fish story. Why stop to tell the president?
If one is halfway lost in a demented woodland,
what about the new book? Any thoughts?
I bet Mr. Wrigley appreciates *that*.

## THE CLOUD OF KNOWING

There are those who would have paid that.
The amount your eyes bonded with
(O spangled home) will have to work it out in a room
like they have certain chairs set up together
which were violet. We all have to fail
at end of days, yet not so pronto
she said. And lo, it was like a breeze of vacuum
beyond the stiff perimeters already granted us.
A whole goes. And then a whole lot.

Most valuably, no one writes a letter
to those sprinting up ahead, who wouldn't read it anyway.
In Dodge and other windswept places
the evening news took pride of place.
Attentats were back. Parental concern loomed. Peckers
swollen by the rainforest beckoned.
Many liberals and even some conservatives
called for a business replacement. Jeez, you guys,
can't you hum anything? What about little Elfrida?
He's not the famous young person I knew.
That one had a lot of little bits in it,
you know, soothing, from home, a minefield.

## CHAFED ELBOWS

A filthy compromise. Pass the planchette.
My friends and I are going to have to leave it here
about the enemy getting married.
And he gave me a whole new list of dodgems to avoid.

The non-jury selection didn't please him
then, nor afterward. No. He doesn't like the shades down.
What do you need doctor appointments for?
Changes of linen are then, as now, optional.
Bernoulli was a Swiss architect. Mathematician, maybe.

## BUNCH OF STUFF

To all events I squirted you
knowing this not to be this came to pass
when we were out and it looked good.
Why wouldn't you want a fresh piece
of outlook to stand in down the years?
See, your house, a former human energy construction,
crashed with us for a few days in May
and sure enough, the polar inscape
brought about some easier poems,
which I guessed was a good thing. At least
some of us were relaxed, Steamboat Bill included.

He didn't drink nothing.
It was one thing
to be ready for their challenge, quite another to accept it.
And if I had a piece of advice for you, this is it:
Poke fun at balm, then suffer lethargy
to irradiate its shallow flood in the new packaging
our enemies processed. They should know.

The Gold Dust twins never stopped supplicating Hoosiers
to limn the trail. There's no Shakespeare.
Through the window, Casanova.
Couldn't get to sleep in the dumb incident
of those days, crimping the frozen feet of Lincoln.

# EAST FEBRUARY

Out there the air is moist I
can tell walking through it.
Thank you so much for coming in.
It's late isn't it,
almost grotesque.
My crew will be in touch.

Not expecting friends
that you don't know yet are coming.
Foxtrot,
performance art,
that I gaze on so fondly today—
this hymn to dowdiness
Howdy-Doody shaped . . .

A mouse can show what works
even if no one knows why, he said.

# HEADING OUT

A single drop fills the rainbow glass.
The fountain overflows. How come the purr
and passing of this every night arrives
at stealth? Just—be prepared. If it happens
every day around this time it happens
more than twice. I'd wager this one has nothing
in it. So's your old man. We get called out
often on all kinds of suspicious business, he decried.
Like when the kittens arrived—*"le grand moment"*—
or when the kitchen sagged with the weight
of the kitchen garden. You and she shouldn't
be out around now, yet nothing I would say
inflects your stalking, be it antelope
or addax, or any number of valuable and not so
permanent entries in the lifestyle sweepstakes.

Some were summoned at the sound of a great drum
and could not put off their walking. Whenever they're drunk
a ghastly change invades the headlines. Here or elsewhere
both rank object and sturdy cult fixture, everything fits,
and finding its place, loses it. Yet so much memory
is stored in this little bin we'd be sure to trip over it
if that were allowed.

I was in here two and a half years.
Missed the inauguration.
Hundreds of witnesses could have sent you the heaviest rain.
I'll go over there sometime and try.
The leader had been staring fervently
like some Lutheran tea party, as though everyone
and his mother was to shut up. Like that.
What's more, the responsibility of that
miscarries when it *is* rubber. Yo, temple!
Hear what I'm sayin'? By the way, have you turned *off* this . . .
Well, I don't know what to tell you about it.
Well I was talking about it, doxology, sockdolager.
On French radio we're trying to take a bad kind of thing
and close up at school.

Own the blankness.
Your napkin ring is bitch-slapping America.
Can't take them out. The place was above all creative.
Do you want these up? Bona-fide curlicues
everyone talks about? The song of mud
learning to handle it?

## FARM HUBBUB

They will always be building buildings.
That time in the good mountains I spent,
flea markets we went to,
their appetizer, chintz. Salvageable mutts.

Anyway, that's what it means.
Don't get all pushed out of shape,
and there she was! Their new technique designed
to stop us, or at least infringe

in some tilapia joint.
Porcelain tools make it alright.
No use, it's fighting again. The great collapsible
retro.

## STUPID PETALS

Remark the comparative zip and panache
of those beautiful hammerhead sharks.
Farther down we get into reptiles,
the "bucket of mud club."

I don't even know if there was a Klondike Scotty.
Lamassu, a protective deity
sketched by Gutzon Borglum, intervened,
twice. And you could . . . one of the top—

Our weatherologist is here.

You're talking to myself—
a slave never forgets its name.
I can put it off right now, summon
your blasphemous magician friend.

So he's not thirty-eight yet.
Sure, Mario had a dentist appointment.
So's your old man run weapons through your eyes.
I wanted to read that book, close the circus.
We don't speak to John again
and there's a lot of them.

Like other millennials I could get you a line.
I wish I had been there!
Days you want to be careful,
you still have to live here.
Shopping wasn't safe. OMG. A Fortuny
slick, basking on uninterested waters,
turns to leave. But it's not over.

# THEREAT

*Kiss me. I'm sick.*

**TODD COLBY**, "Friday and Baffled"

Nothing wrong with you, just
get me arrested,
because when you haven't seen someone, nights become very respectful.
Hers were not usually submitted to
in our living room.
Just rub your hands there.

Fie, Cagliostro!
We circled down, rules are honey.
Is that a blackwatch,
a noticeable gift
to the hall where too much happens?
You are the whole in your tight truths.
You need all 27 of 'em.
Convenient here last night,
the lemon on the archduke . . .
What is he, a fuzzy, jumping old man?
Exact living requires that you talk to but don't even touch me.
Professional raiders interpret all of it.
When do they turn them over?

Quiet and adversarial at once,
a lifeless man, they say.
Onward to Christian bathrooms,
weak continuity, wok celerity or celebrity.
Good lurk. You'll look back on heavy rain and think
you were kept from enjoying us and thrusting.

Let the birds run with the trees!
A beautiful day and
marine historians
complained we're all safe, from there on in,
of innocent people's headaches.
Once stapled correctly to your uncle,
scones are seduced.
Forget any mistranslations,
miscommunications. The past
loves you, baby.
Go sandpaper a horse.

## ELEVENTH PLEASANTRY

Once the giant tickler is out of your system
its equipment equivalent will be brought to you.
Use it for goatseed.

Two solutions:
plagiarizes his own authors. For shame!
Dopey music all the time.

All those don't render the house unresonant.
Do what I can
in this unsuccessful world.

Don't smile that way.

## RAMBLING STATEMENT

You can go out and talk to someone
or pick at your face,
working through these issues.
Move in with us!

Kitchen police talked about getting ready,
the way it was intended to be.
Any muscles would have stood out at that horse.

Tacoburger counseling, all that spunky food,
the Christmas tree ... Where did that go?
Pettifoggery, or not? Catalyst construction
continued about two feet away.
They used it for language
that somebody said once. Don't answer it.
Leave things where they are.

Customs, *douane*,
displays of llama-butter, stingy-pretty.
Your deductible!

He was famous for riding around town in a black hat.
He suffered a long time ago,
and will love you forever.

# THE ENTHUSIASTS

That building has won over everything.
Here in high school opportunities are numerous,
but what are they *for*?
You could live like a girl of thirteen
in a single dream,
quash outside solicitations,
go back to sleep every time.

*This* is outside, and remiss:
It takes tools to deploy the core of your dream,
face a common ford others have crossed too,
on Saratoga waters, now and again imbibing
notes of lemongrass and coconut.
I told him we don't get anything from North Dakota.
Bilingual bullying was on the next floor.

We had the most beautiful morning and afternoon. We just had lunch
    with
Dean Pavlov's proxy; the entire breeze,
right on the tabletop here.
They're not going to sue their money,
accident waiting to happen, which you would need anyway.
Leonard doesn't take himself for just anybody.

*Ah, ça alors! Mais pas du tout!*
A very good guide, no doubt,
bringing up fine images in the guts of the past.
Occupy it by dint of occupying it.
I was saying that to you when
plotting new frescoes:
It was a comestible kind of love.
Get in and learn something.

Go smack into Mrs. Duvet. The heart's buildings—
simply ripping. Half a building up
(and we need many), lock yourself in
the lugubrious gondola. He was
just standing over there,
talking to them.

## DRAMEDY

Things I left on your paper:
One of the craziest episodes that ever overtook me.
Do you like espionage? A watered charm?
My pod cast aside, I'll walk in the human street,
protect the old jib from new miniseries.

I could swear it moved
in incomplete backyards
to endorse the conversation, request to be strapped in.
Then it will be time to take the step
giving fragile responses,
and finally he wrote the day.

It happened in the water
so that was nice.

It comes ready conflated:
vanilla for get lost, flavor of the time
of his sponsor's destiny. Be on that sofa.

I was crossing the state line as they were reburying the stuff.
You break the time lock, the bride's canister . . .
but we did say that we'd be back.

## THE UNDEFINABLE JOURNEY

Where do you think you're
going to get lines to
punish the stranger with?
Cursing, destiny's piñata;
it's a surprise! (Partly sunny.)

O neat-o friend of mine,
to add a central target to the
mix is not to chase sea
monsters, real or imagined.

*You* drop the floor.
Small white chicken friends,
like life itself
over time last night . . .
And, what have you done with this one?

# THE PIE DISTRICT

This is what we need to do
at a certain point (wait for it,
effendi): examine cheesy knockoffs
of dubious provenance. Are we ready to help yet?

Four negatives make a positive. I even joined city hall.
Waves of attentiveness and straight A's followed,
but I was so crestfallen, the ship's little
dog seemed to think so. It
hung around impetuously.

They're the ones to get
somebody to do things, pick up
after him. We'll see who finishes soon
in shock.

There was nothing not to like about
the new self-monitoring system. Yet strangely,
the pie district voted against it.
I, however, custodian of sang-froid, made
a 180-degree swivel. The bandoneon
keeps its goofy elixir
locked in its dark depths.

Thank you, by the way.

I saw the daughter of his king and illustrator,
Mrs. Walter H. Browne, streaking past the hedges
sparkling with dew, just as if it were another time.
Lizzie! Lizzie Browne!, I stammered. But she took
no notice of me, or the hundred or so other guests
gathered on the lawn to salute spring.
This *is* ominous.
And yet, I managed to gasp,
I'll have more of it for breakfast.
Two things that went up and never
came back. I don't understand.
That must have been about drinking,
feline intrigue. Can I go to my doctor now?

The fan kid's still chewing on a Fifth Avenue bar,
which they may not make anymore
with or without 'tude.

It's been three years now . . .
That's just it—we don't know!
Do it the hard way.

And we go out and visit.

## DOMANI, DOPODOMANI

Once in a while a message arrives here
from friends we haven't seen in some time.
Family members try to reach us
to ask about old questions. Finally, each of us
has some concern or other.

I can hear the signs breaking up.
To have half-lived in a balloon to Fresno
solves it, at least for now. Different . . .
at home. After we've been in town a few days
and may have moved, anywhere but within easy reach,
this is kissing's only surface. Midday suction.
It's savory—let's devour,
or do something about it, rusty at the bottom
before we came to this past.

It was a moment, what can I say.

# THE GOOFIAD

Um, it wasn't my project
to prise them apart.
Pale Jessica had come full circle.
Case in point: She spelled one application
under presidential law. How it became
one of the names one can't recall.

But on the other hand
good old people
watch the convention.
It's guaranteed,
and not be president.
People had yet to live

and believe your own cameras
which it probably isn't going to,
picking up the same thing. Premium hype,
it's off-ladle. While out driving in my car
repeating both of them,
we'll pull together and,
kind of interesting
that I heard you fix a lot more concentrated . . .

It was all anybody could do.
The garter store fell through the cracks,
or if there was another way
I didn't know you were ticklish—
with a little note which said
Sing something subtle and insinuating.
Aunts go to jail.
On the facial committee equipment,
a woman by the name of Lottie Timms.

This is the traditional way not to kiss at all.

I'm really not into the past, a zoo.
Really not. Why are you doing that for me?
Urinal my dreams, it seems. I could think of something,
the angle of his shirt, perhaps. The shatterproof screen door . . .

Elsewhere in real cities, a few biographies point,
postulate. The rare setback school holds.
I saw young, freelancing, orange-juice-in-the-desert,
mythical ladies of China (another of those countries)
fallen together. I wouldn't send her away.

Don't get on a train like this
(twisting one of her legs). You're very liberal.
(Well, I suppose so. It's something I imagined.)

You'd better decide what not to do.
Everything is pop-up, my 3-time advisor said.
He holds my ear. I'll be quite honest with you about it.
A man alive, please welcome him.
Decent New Yorkers said I can't go his way. He . . .
Supposedly I'm president! A wretch like me!

I hadn't heard the word.

## DICKIE'S BORDER VACATION

Nobody knows whether I should stay here with you.
The comics became devoted after his mother died.
Cross mentoring, peer checking, peer coaching were brought on,
with beans and leftovers. Like most books, this one puts
a damper on me. On Sundays I used to populate,

they were running out of steam but didn't know it.
Now we like it. My face is too young. Later, politics
would trample our undeveloped theses.

Professor, I'm going to set you up again.
Don't wheeze next time. Railroad elders
would border on the interesting.
What of Lepchek, Spongey, Mr. Johnson? Huntz Hall?
These and others, swept to their doom over the solid-seeming railing,
make for clouded sailing ahead. I'm going to start working on it,
or the other. A rumble upstate said, "No, they're not.
I told them eighty-six hundred times. You got enough feet
to refer to, now, with mixed success. A drop in pressure,
wine and fripperies, is what I can do for you, drab gent."

Do you want to eat those sunny, idle cakes?
If I can get a cancellation

to feign grand illness, alas, he likes to take care of
each other. And I think, I really do think that
a poultice . . . Hey, I've been hungry for two seconds.
You're staying without a gift. A lot of liquid
from Latin hands will trickle down to the strange Oz house
I affirmed to get back out of business.
Morning glories, poppies . . . and they keep saying they want to hire.
Me? Oh, I saw him throwing a glass of water around,
told him not to participate. Whom did you involve?

The Alps are for women, strictly speaking.
It is definitely possible, in the Slovak station,
to not be too sorry for her or she would be putting up with it.
Well, you don't want it to. Perhaps no outcome,
but impeccably located, shocking images
in forests of creosote, making an event possible. It's special-loaded
with mind-chips for the tri-state area. Dirt all election day.

We made so much money this is almost on the house.
It was 1910.

# A FOUNTAIN IN THE STREET

A *pregnant ant circles the drain.*
**LARRY FAGIN**, "Content Is a Glimpse"


The fountain is dead.
The meadows aren't open
for reasons best known to themselves,
in case you asked.

The refrigerator on the porch liked it.
So, too, did Mrs. Roosevelt.
Everybody's been so wonderful—
more access, more experiences.

Fact: the Badger State is composed of ferns
and feathers. Wild rice grows there. The natives
harvest it in boats, banging the stems with poles
so it falls off and covers the floor of the boat.

# THE UNDESERVING RIVER

The tour we went on was a house, actually.
Kittens lived behind its clapboards,
rarely issuing forth for food.
A whole other hierarchy of beings
was established there, who saw little need
to attend to business, e.g., a letterhead.

At times around four o'clock a leaf pile
would get blown by the wind.
Except for that the weather was mild
especially by comparison with what we thought
we had already experienced
in harder times, when things were just so.

Gym equipment was underutilized, as always.
In my notes I had three or four things I wanted
to draw to your attention, but it no longer seems
important. I'll go out the way I came in,
incidentally wishing you and yours a happy Christmas
while we go visit our parent-kids
versus the people of Missouri
and Raymond Verandah and his orchestra,
and turn up again. Be that way!

The man said you needed a —
and he may have been right.
Here, I'll bring it over.

*Skipper takes credit.*
Well, let's hope so.
The knotted reply
come clear tomorrow morning.
That didn't seem to be true.

In the white shirt, less than a year ago,
minute entries blown together
weed house sleep with men
comes after not too bad.

Married folks prefer the texasburger.
That was in August,
freeway caucuses,
semiofficial, dun dugs.
The man said you needed a

to gain more customers.
Less than a year ago

a giant crab
in the sky above Tokyo
whispers compassion—

I know not what minds have fled,
*Eheu!*
Short of remembering can you rate the coughs?

And some of you are dead.
Violence on the terrain.

Where you headed for?

## BY GUESS AND BY GOSH

O awaken with me
the inquiring goodbyes.
Ooh what a messy business
a tangle and a muddle
(and made it seem quite interesting).

He ticks them off:
leisure top,
a different ride home,
whispering, in a way,
whispered whiskers,
so many of the things you have to share.

But I was getting on,
and that's what you don't need.
I'm certainly sorry about scaring your king,
if indeed that's what happened to him.
You get Peanuts and War and Peace,
some in rags, some in jags, some in
velvet gown. They want
the other side of the printing plant.

There were concerns.
Say hi to jock-itch, leadership principles,
urinary incompetence.
Take that, perfect pitch.
And say a word for the president,
for the scholar magazines, papers, a streaming.
Then you are interested in poetry.

## FLOWERS, RESTORATION

Yes, the great residential palaces,
the porter's station on Pitz Palu—
it all makes sense. Intentional? Me lie here
with bonny complications from sometimes,
the kind you wear.
                    Her wide shoulders were born.


The cleanup effort extended far beyond today's tousled landscape.
What good did it do if everybody was away, on business, mostly
trying out olive oil shampoo? Aye, true geezers paced
the measured mile, in touch with my father's
distinguished postal service, a flight risk
for the several hours it remained on sale,
their co-producer.
                    Anybody to take care of yourself
breathes in the challenge. First I'm gonna brush my teef.
What happens next is anybody's mess.
And, I might add, a real treat knowing you.

## BLUEPRINTS AND OTHERS

The man across the street seems happy,
or pleased. Sometimes a porter evades the grounds.
After you play a lot with the military
you are my own best customer.

I've done five of that.
Make my Halloween. Ask me not to say it.
The old man wants to see you — *now*.
That's all right, but find your own.
Do you want to stop using these?

Last winning people told me to sit on the toilet.
Do not put on others what you can put on yourself.
*How to be in the city my loved one.*
Men in underwear ... A biography field
like where we live in the mountains,

a falling. Yes, I know you have.
Troves of merchandise, you know, "boomer buzz."
Hillbilly sculptures of the outside.
(They won't see anybody.)

# SUPERCOLLIDER

Past the gaga experiments
to ginger high school thriller days
I wheel fragile issues: a fight on there,
bulbous antennae, a herald
carved alone in the archer position—sweet!

We had a few people over to
celebrate the monotony of the new place.
Meatless meat loaf. Roger. Over to

you. I took a piece of plain foolscap,
my American University in Baku stationery,
sole thing to be underestimated here,
and set down just words that wrote something,
probably as close as I want to keep to it,

all the water and stringiness.
It feels like Sunday today
but it's Saturday. What does Saturday feel like
on Sunday? Not that it's that
hard to remember—I'd always be grinning and opened.

No protocol; heck, no manners
on flood watch. She's one of the famed Gowanus sisters.
It hasn't affected the weather yet.

Do you get a sense of white table settings,
the so-called vacant stare that afflicts them
as adults on a sit-down strike?

Listen up, tenderfoot. Who says you need to be awake
to appreciate poetry? The landlady, that's who.

Where are they now?

# SEPARATE HEARINGS

## 1

We'll put a hundred million dollars over the
Brno chair
that I remembered seeing it
after they couldn't find them
The principle of a lifetime

The oft-embargoed news—
You gonna do it now?
In 1946
these men and all women
First
they won't see anybody

## 2

Already attempted, is not gonna hold you in there
The governor had an issue with it
eating their supplies

Any day is yesterday
one of Dad's geraniums
no more than a foot away
looking sane
and reveal herself just a little bit
had been there for at least nine years

hope you haven't done anything outside

# RUFFLE THEORY

I'm the wardrobe expert.
Electrocuted! You can't mean that.
All those years nothing but his blond
ticking hair, and vote for him. Whomever.
And then we never did hear much from him.

He saw Henry Gray
and came up over the road
with money you collected.
Start running around,
otherwise it won't get done at all.

That's just right reason, burning all the time,
soothing, temporary relief.
Handsome and blue-eyed
is what I'm talking about.
Did we mention sensational?

For me, those emigrants last,
a bundle of windows.
Kind of grief-stricken, were they?
He was having an emergency,
just what's on this morning.
No word on whether reverse psychology worked.

## THE PRICE OF EGGS

No one remembers Mr. Coffee Nerves,
his lap of beads, allegedly sitting there.

Families with pets, help me with this.
Something may disturb him:
sun's parody, the price of eggs, raw orange.

Who was that plant from?
She, somewhat evaporated . . . Would I laugh?
You are not to be concerned about fish.
Extreme ants polished our definition.

In the hooded phase, a second ago.
She may have broken loose
only among the treatises of those provided for,
and work behind them
for dandies, for a princess,
trained buggers:
"*Up to 13½ million pounds of dry goods sold.*"

## ALL THAT, AND MORE

Suddenly I couldn't believe
you have to put it back,
must be intelligent,
bring sandwich money,
whether British or American.

We couldn't get enough cakes in our family,
something to make it worthwhile, some stance.
You like making amends, isn't it?
Throw the book at him.

It was nice everywhere else.
A Caribbean shithole documentary told him
softly, as in an evening sunset,
into an emotional atmosphere
happy from gay.
They say I hit the neck, thank you,
down under the covers.
If I'd Google . . .

Put eye drops in
into my personal window, dapper Fred said.

He pressed the healed corollary
(this was after all his day away)
with the accuracy of a speed knife
putting and placing on the line again
all foretold by Becky Mushroom,
leaving us walking into afternoon.
It was chaos like that
past our striated feet.

Gimme a break!
No I don't feel used,
though I have a less than human face.
The usual definition of fun is:
quite comfortable when they are.

When you were happening to him,
Nineteen barrels for five nights a week.

You've fallen, roof,
graphite and herbs, having a good time with us.
Deluxe your pilot right now.
Dr. Stinkhandler, this feeling of helplessness:
all that, and more,
all hunched over,
over-egged,
frumpier lamb symptoms.

Then pile it on
like you wouldn't believe!
The pretty pieces,
a hundred salads,
that led to the eye doctor,
which led to the spa
(dangerous water).

There are four physical engineers
(if you don't want something expensive on your writing table)
could cauterize a tank,

qualify for the purchase.
We stopped yesterday with some pamphlets,
overturned it to his grief.
The story got mentioned.
(Used to have scraps).

## WARM REGARDS

*i remember today like it was yesterday.*
GARRETT CAPLES, "Love Is Made of Sky"


You want to think about it:
Everybody's frantic but Bob.
A tunnel from under
gave him a folded-up photo of Dad.
I'll get you there
and provide you with the little you know
to measure somebody.

I'm not hanging out with you,
generous to a fault.
Buy 'em large, when we talk
about foot sizes.
Somebody said it was about ten.
He didn't say it didn't,
and it would be there
for maybe half an hour.
Do you want it?

There's some type of instructions in
November last year.

In Nerva Scotia people lost one every night,
been out there shaking.
Don't think that you want to get out.

The young men are building a boat.
Definitely a freedom container.
That's what he does.

*Ordered some wine.*
*It was right around here,*
*replaced by a little kid*
*come to see what you're gettin' at.*
*We'll requisition 'em.*

There were preconditions.
This is unusual, morphs into
these other things, this modern age,
a lot of finishing up to do.

# THE HONOR ROLL

Jake came lurching toward me.
Was it this month?
No, it was last month.
I see. Then why did I leave the research open?
As you came along the hall
I thought of a lot of things,
then this day, Valentine's Day,
which it isn't but there are a lot of big spare pumps around.

## A NEW DESIRE

Not so good anymore,
post avant-garde. How's that?
Find anybody still puzzled up.
Your marcelled feet were on the stage:

If you could save our container
in Pennsylvania in October . . .
The fire broke out/declared itself.
We drank the grass, drunken fish,
in servile mode. An antique something about it.

You'll have to pay for brunch—I'm too excited.
Milk and carrots from the editor at
my beloved Sierras!
It passed inspection,
or they'll have found that too:
Fully understand
(gonna close some time,
pudgy rules, hyper airlines,
lifter-upper—a boomlet, so he said).

There goes another one belies
any significant pores,
and everyone at home, officials stressed.

Don't slide down the ones John says they still aren't using—
the worst driveway in
western Connecticut.
He's right—it shouldn't do anything,
culprit shoes. Why many have passed on to the sun.

## HOMESCHOOLED

That was never an issue.
That is, it was and it wasn't.

I'm supposed to be angry about something.
Only you know what it is,
born ahead of time.

Headbangers, all.
You have to have some Elmer's crayon juice.

Did you want to hang out a little bit first
at my house
we were just talking about?

The quiet street is flagged.
He gets into everything.

I used to sing a song
he tried a few months ago,
explains Billy.
No, it just happened that way,

the new boxy silhouettes.

I'm in touch with you and I'm not going to let you go.

Stay off that leg.

## THE SPONGE OF SLEEP

Why waver? He won't stab me for
when we sat down widely pixillated
between the horizon and the lice.
We're off to the sea, someone said.
Let's direct it to us
and our various enjoyment. I hate it when
we're made of snot one
minute, stone so simple the next.
I would think first,
and then we were there,
sooner other than that.

All this could have been avoided if
we aren't doing anything.
Serviceberry shot down by squirrels,
you don't have to thank everybody.
The charm of abuse sings in ways we are not.
Or we can sit and travel, aimless ceremony.
I paint feet. Summer pants. A wave of translation
on the apples, like the friendly air out there.
If they do so, they do so disproportionately
to his three-year-old brother-in-law,

who patted the expats in a purgatorial whisper.
The inside of the crate had expanded exponentially
from carrying one load of artichokes.

Be one of those on whom nothing is lost, advises Henry.
Well, OK. I'm awake. No problem
that I can see, unless it's running out of raw material,
like his dog Jerry opted out of the transubstantiation process.
It was ever thus:

Cabochon pluots weighted down with
*ananas en belle vue*. They drank Salada tea
in a statement.
We just gotta keep that stranded one safe as before,
and getting out of here.
How far is the Old Log Inn?
I'd love to read it.
The woods are sorry for them.
Small rain will land somewhere.

# COLORS

You should see through the ride.
At least that is the argument I've been hearing,
a misery at every time of night
including ghost calculus.

Yep what a story.
Keep on the trails
and of course, if you roll it all out right at the start, you've got
leftover motives to account for the window signature.

Maybe even some other decimal system? Who said not to elaborate when
    there's a surplus
of evidence? Not the man in the moon, surely. Steady compromise.

Been reading *The Hole in the Blanket* by Mr. Completely, already hailed
    for his seminal *The*
*Spot on the Wall.* I don't know if you ever tried to.

Telethon, once it starts
we get answers phoned in from all over.
David's not worried, and if he's
not worried, nobody else should be either.

*Banner with strange device . . .*

Locker-room privacy. Since many have different opinions,
rob its family member.
Liberty Hall, indeed.

## GRAVY FOR THE PRISONERS

I wouldn't try to capture it
on the page, or in a blog, the inauspicious
leavings of a day. Closer to dream
than the hum of streets, and people
who once walked along them.

Yeah, I know. Know what I'm saying?
The grounds were ultimately too large for the compound.
A tree takes flight, and patterns are coaxed
into recurring on adjacent walls,
out of thin air.
No such titan ever visited
during my days as aedile. Yet wisps
still buttonhole us in random moats:
Was it this you were expecting,
and if not, why not?

# GLOVE COMPARTMENT

*"Did they mention a shawl?"*
NICOLAS HUNDLEY, "Gothic Novel"


For treasonable us
we sold my brotherhood down the stream.

I'm always surprised at
how green-tempered you are

toward other, frog-related chains
of weeks, or months, or

whatever you call them.
He devoted Christmas day to finding out

all the news about Mama and their three puppies.
The foundry was out and would have to be relit,

nineteen years is enough. It's not
overcrowded until the day we go to the farm places'

blank pill.
Silence is everywhere, like silence,

is suspect, she being . . .
We'll try to get home

throughout the air.
I don't want to have to speak to you again

and have to unveil
you called her.

Can't they stay generated?
We're not going to start today

because that is awesome
which in turn stirs up the system and

we are ready and we're still not smart.
Put it up a little

to the great cleansing wind,
a gay, fat guest

or getting my train elected.
Can I be a medicine?

The innocence collected now
that's not, interestingly enough,

the easiest way to do it, is
her suit

sent me a bunch of little . . .
Let my song fill your heart. It's

more than I wanted.
I had always wanted to do just the

right thing and fit in with the.
From more dishonest fences loomed the percent.

I didn't have leave to be
the only justice that gets through.

It's so exhausting being a
medium, especially the 94th military one.

Atta bugger ... He belongs in passports now
the productivity panel has its view.

Undressing her was unfunny
biscuit routine.

His share of the opera
betokens carriages.

Just can't live anymore.
Always happy to shoot the breeze.

## PUSHOVER

Moreover, they'd like to have
at least an important committee.
Whispers should plainly open up.
Next, a tax on everything.

Does that make sense?
It's when your father was formed.
There's the weather and all those dogs or something.
Space could only hurt him
or agree with him.

Moving on, to western Coney Island,
sprawling temperatures suggest
we apologize for any inconvenience.

Or you could chew on it another time.

## HONESTLY,

we could send you out there
to join the cackle squad,
but hey, that highly accomplished,
thinly regarded equestrian—well there was no way
he was going to join the others' field trip.
Wouldn't put his head on the table.
But here's the thing:

They had owned great dread,
knew of a way to get away from here
through ice and smoke
always clutching her fingers, like it says
to do.

Once we were passionate about the police,
yawned in the teeth of pixels,
but a far rumor blanked us out.
We bathed in moonshine.
Now, experts disagree.
Were we unhappy or sublime?

We'll have to wait until the next time
an angel comes rapping at the door
to rejoice docently.

(I know there's a way to do this.)

## FRONT AND PEARL

This time it set off a lemon telenovela.
Chickens bolted—bummer!
Just then the buzzer sounded.
No subtle docks ministered to it.

No longer pudgy, all get off free.
It was "a regular rout," she encouraged.
Sweet alyssum, you see, just doesn't cut it for me.
The Wall Street crash of 1929
hit us both hard.

That would be a fine way to conduct things,
to bring it here, referring to the doctor.
The long Hudson Valley flows along
beside it, the river I mean.

She was the lemon target of reality.
Here, I'll do the butcher.
Yes, the sun has officially set
until tomorrow.
The cathedral had an unfinished look to it.

What will you dream of,
two months after we breathed?
I don't know but what he'd
cut us for the longest time.

Glance through your tendonitis sheaf.
You'll find everything in order
and turn up again.
The nurses are getting nervous.

## PSYCHIC BITTERS

Did he describe the blue stripe again,
unelected governor?
And from trees to hospitals, one story
perfectly formed suddenly entered into eternal rest.

They won't have any additional
waves around the hotel,
who won't have been here long enough
because somebody got the idea,
nor would a duck deal with holiday baking and the like.

# A DRUGSTORE IN DULUTH

Rejiggered, shy as I was, after thinking I've won
it came to pass there were no more attentive gestures.

That may be part of the joke. Restaurants will reopen,
many buried in the county exit. Be not beseeched.

Door muscles, an unholy fragrance borders the faces on the tree.
An inspector on a leash rinsed the iconostasis.

From the electric counties
I sent it with his clothes.

O happy gloom! Besotted with interiors,
Dutch still lifes circle the pole.

## SAMBA HÉROÏQUE

You would probably know them
if you were stressed.
You were nice, safe, and strong.

These things get appreciated,
unearned, unfathomed.
But last night he wasn't so happy about it.
Joining us in a statement is
the former governor, arrested,
asserted, in melted fruition,
to be crisply doomed,
not for a long, long time.

Don't touch this stuff.
It was a debate, unless—
of this, that, and the other.
Drunks in the night, arctic suburb,
party in an igloo.

I exercise seeking a lance
here or there,

like any sauce or syrup.
You would probably know them if you
were stressed. And not be able to know that.
That's what *you* believe.

## POSITION PAPER

This is my outfit.
Government spooks did the rest. Didn't you know?
Not really. No one is in a hairier place,
my flat mountain.

I'm going to have dinner some night on the ropes.

Bottom line, no one was killed.
That way you retain ownership.
Droopy night brought on by the
old gray mold makers. It was quite . . . unexpected.
That's why I think it's so important
the way squat noses learn, and fast.

Okeydoke, I'll tell you in maple shade.
Fast forward to the beginning of your Christmas present.
I have to turn this down,
to clean his pipes,
or clock, whatever.

That's a healing dressing
how many years late —

the continuous way to do it. Sorry. My dizzy.
Pulled pork sliders clogged the glee gate.

No one was killed.

Having a nightgown
under the armpits, darling? Dirt and dare
can be forgiven eyeballing the toiletry lottery
whose torque proclaims it other.

## FORGET WHERE I HEARD IT

With pigeon force the air men
come clattering. It would be sad
if it wasn't so funny, one swore.

Stay out of the nettles.
Do not live above the shop.
His men may find you there.
Otherwise, as coma says, my beans, my peas, my coma
get read into the riot act.

That comes later.

After three decades of futility, you have to ask:
Who was this composer?
Was he known for anything else?
Is the mere survival of the notes justified,
or do we all survive this way, more or less?

## CHEAP LEGS

His wives liked him.
To be comfortable in his facial hair
is as much and as little of a man
as one can ask.

Languid articles you don't know where
are what brought us to the party,
exchanged trivial sorrow for one big one
just as the old man had predicted.
The moon, daubed an inauspicious hue,
that night, was determined to see it through,
"make an end run around darkness,"
someone said.
                    As long as there were two
of them, it didn't matter, or mattered
in another way, like momentum.

And who's to say we didn't gradually understand
our situation, along with everyone else's?
The way a whole city, standing, radiates glee?

The morning after, that's who.

exurb. What were you driving at (when you said): Used to joke I'm in the retirement business. The snow is beginning to fall again. I'm wondering whether I should go out. How can you give orders when nobody is listening? A friend and two boys. Here where love was quiet it was possible to think discontinuously of the folds ahead, faith on a tricycle. Only it. Or she got a hole in her dress. It was a million to one it was something bad. The windows rattled as the train swept through at breakfast.

You may want to rethink that decision. Bother the others . . . It was right there in his military book. You wood have too oracle snow. You knew that. Everybody did. My dynasty, confessions of a lily from wire. That was a terrible thing to do purely naked. Grovelling conditions apply, not to go all agony aunt on you. You're not ready for this. No poet is, only you already came. The crane doesn't know if the weather will return. I don't want it. I don't give a shit. Something that would have fell . . . the potato orchard with attached oriental kitchen.

They don't say please in heaven. All business is carried out in the prenoon hours, leaving time for naps and reflection. This is the kind of life I was supposed to lead. What happened? you ask. Cutie pie went bye bye. Once the hypnotic hour of twelve has struck you are like any other paying guest, waiting for the intoxicating smell of burgers to waft up the stairway.

When Doc moved back to our area he noticed the wretched smiles, legacy of our previous god. Who, he wondered, enjoys this kind of ambiance. And sure enough, it was Independence Day. And word went out: It's the right day but the wrong month. Go back to sleep. And they did (writing in the grass). The Fuller Brush man (clean-jawed) stopped by. See you down there. Lemme know. Just because Scooby Doo thinks you should . . .

Dirt officials implied a small little BOMB. And sleep, trying to find them. Now I approve not just initiative A-1 3 but the whole dumb panoply, Uncle Ralph. Sign me up for festooned. They say she was last seen by a lake, crying.

You knew that. Everybody did.

## A SWEET DISORDER

Pardon my sarong. I'll have a Shirley Temple.
Certainly, sir. Do you want a cherry with that?
I guess so. It's part of it, isn't it?
Strictly speaking, yes. Some of them likes it,
others not so much. Well, I'll have a cherry.
I can be forgiven for not knowing it's de rigueur.
In my commuter mug, please. Certainly.

He doesn't even remember me.
It was a nice, beautiful day.
One of your favorite foxtrots was on,
neckties they used to wear.
You could rely on that.

My gosh, it's already 7:30.
Are these our containers?
Pardon my past, because, you know,
it was like all one piece.
It can't have escaped your escaped your attention
that I would argue.
How was it supposed to look?
Do I wake or sleep?

## ACKNOWLEDGMENTS

The author gratefully acknowledges the following publications in which poems in *Breezeway* first appeared, sometimes in slightly different form: *The American Reader, augustone2013, The Awl, Believer, Berkeley Poetry Review, BOMB, Boston Review, Cordite Poetry Review, Denver Quarterly, Fence, Flaunt, Frieze, Granta, Hyperallergic, The Iowa Review, jubilat, London Review of Books, Maggy, The Nation, New Walk, The New York Review of Books, The New Yorker, The Paris Review, PEN Poetry Series, PN Review, Poetry, Prelude, T: The New York Times Style Magazine, The Times Literary Supplement, The Volta,* and *The White Review.*

"Andante and Filibuster" was published in *Privacy Policy: The Anthology of Surveillance Poetics,* edited by Andrew Ridker (Boston: Black Ocean, 2014).

"Hand with a Picture" was commissioned by the Smithsonian Institution's National Portrait Gallery for the catalogue of its 2014–15 exhibition *Face Value: Portraiture in the Age of Abstraction.*

"Homeschooled" first appeared in the program booklet produced for the 2013 Poetry International Festival Rotterdam (Netherlands).

"Honestly," first appeared in the Academy of American Poets' "Poem-a-Day" e-mail series.

On the following pages, a stanza break occurs at the bottom of the page (not including pages on which the break is evident because of the regular stanzaic structure of the poem): 4, 8, 19, 36, 39, 41, 45, 49, 52, 61, 67, 72, 77, 79, 83, 93.

## ABOUT THE AUTHOR

John Ashbery was born in Rochester, New York, in 1927. He earned degrees from Harvard and Columbia, and went to France as a Fulbright Scholar in 1955, living there for much of the next decade. His many collections of poetry include *Quick Question* (2012), *Planisphere* (2009) and *Notes from the Air: Selected Later Poems* (2007), which was awarded the 2008 International Griffin Poetry Prize. *Self-Portrait in a Convex Mirror* (1975) won the three major American prizes—the Pulitzer, the National Book Award, and the National Book Critics Circle Award—and an early book, *Some Trees* (1956) was selected by W. H. Auden for the Yale Younger Poets Series. The Library of America published the first volume of his collected poems in 2008. A two-volume set of his collected translations from the French (poetry and prose) was published in 2014. Active in various areas of the arts throughout his career, he has served as executive editor of *Art News* and as art critic for *New York* magazine and *Newsweek*; he exhibits his collages at the Tibor de Nagy Gallery (New York). He taught for many years at Brooklyn College (CUNY) and Bard College, and in 1989–90 delivered the Charles Eliot Norton lectures at Harvard. He is a member of the American Academy of Arts and Letters (receiving its Gold Medal for Poetry in 1997) and the American Academy of Arts and Sciences, and was a chancellor of the Academy of American Poets from 1988 to 1999. The winner of many prizes and awards, both nationally and internationally, he has received two Guggenheim Fellowships and was a MacArthur Fellow from 1985 to 1990; recently, he received the Medal for Distinguished Contribution to American Letters from the National Book Foundation (2011) and a National Humanities Medal, presented by President Obama at the White House (2012). His work has been translated into more than twenty-five languages. He lives in New York. Additional information is available in the "About John Ashbery" section of the Ashbery Resource Center's website, a project of The Flow Chart Foundation, www.flowchartfoundation.org/arc.